Love Behind the Lines

a Night Stalkers 5E romance story
by
M. L. Buchman

Copyright 2016 Matthew Lieber Buchman
Published by Buchman Bookworks

All rights reserved.
This book, or parts thereof,
may not be reproduced in any form
without permission from the author.
Discover more by this author at:
www.mlbuchman.com

Cover images:
Interracial Couple Being Intimate In Front Of Window © Rocketclips | Dreamstime.com

Buchman Bookworks

Other works by M.L. Buchman

The Night Stalkers

Main Flight
The Night Is Mine
I Own the Dawn
Wait Until Dark
Take Over at Midnight
Light Up the Night
Bring On the Dusk
By Break of Day

White House Holiday
Daniel's Christmas
Frank's Independence Day
Peter's Christmas
Zachary's Christmas
Roy's Independence Day

and the Navy
Christmas at Steel Beach
Christmas at Peleliu Cove

5E
Target of the Heart
Target Lock on Love

Firehawks

Main Flight
Pure Heat
Full Blaze
Hot Point
Flash of Fire

SMOKEJUMPERS
Wildfire at Dawn
Wildfire at Larch Creek
Wildfire on the Skagit

Delta Force
Target Engaged
Heart Strike

Angelo's Hearth
Where Dreams are Born
Where Dreams Reside
Maria's Christmas Table
Where Dreams Unfold
Where Dreams Are Written

Eagle Cove
Return to Eagle Cove
Recipe for Eagle Cove
Longing for Eagle Cove
Keepsake for Eagle Cove

Deities Anonymous
Cookbook from Hell: Reheated
Saviors 101

Dead Chef Thrillers
Swap Out!
One Chef!
Two Chef!

SF/F Titles
Nara
Monk's Maze

1

***"Mission recall. Repeat, mission** recall."*

"You've got to be shitting me." Lieutenant Manfred "M&M" Malcolm looked down at the radio to make sure that it was on tonight's frequency and that the message wasn't for someone else.

"I'm only three goddamn klicks out!" He shouted at the radio, though he didn't hit his transmit key to send his least fond regards. There were some places that American military helicopters should never be caught and he was in one of them. His Little Bird MH-6 might be stealth rigged and his radio signal encrypted…

but that wouldn't make him or the point of origin of any electronic transmission invisible.

"Mission X-ray Tango Alpha is aborted," the Air Mission Commander repeated. "Return to base."

XTA. Extraction of prime target Alpha. That was his mission tonight.

"Goddamn it!" He hated the alphabet agencies. DIA, NSA, and most particularly the CIA. They never seemed to know what they wanted. In the military, you received a mission, you planned it, and you by god executed it after you were given the "Go!" order. In the CIA he figured they had a mission board and flung darts at it until they hit something and said, "Oh, let's do that." He'd bet they wore blindfolds while planning or whatever it was they did back in Langley. After that, because shit flowed downhill, it would be:

"Hey Manny," as if pretending they were already on a first-name basis before they'd even talked and he didn't have a rank after a decade of flying and even facing down Officer Candidate School. "We have a top level asset"—which meant spy—"whose cover is blown. We need an immediate extraction. Tonight."

There were only two companies in the entire US military able to fly a route like the one needed, SOAR's 5D and his own 5E. The helicopters of the Special Operations Aviation Regiment's 5th Battalion E Company had been in a better position so he'd been sent in.

Now he was deep behind Russian lines—except the Russians still insisted they weren't in Crimea—and he had to figure out how to get back without tripping some high-tech booby trap. All that noise about the Russians being so far behind in tech was just that, noise. Their problem was that they couldn't afford as much of the good shit as America could, but what they had was damned impressive. And those heavy-duty assets were concentrated in places of particular importance to the Russian government…like every square meter within a hundred klicks of his present position just outside of Sevastopol, Crimea. Which had been part of the Ukraine until recently. He wished it still was, because then he'd be welcome instead of being a target.

Low and fast had been his answer going in; he just hoped that it would work equally well on his passage out. He yanked up on the collective and shoved the cyclic forward to lay the hammer down hard.

That hope lasted almost thirteen seconds.

Some Russian soldier with an itchy trigger finger and thirty-year old technology fired a missile at his trace. It was a crazy waste of $100,000 *Igla* surface-to-air missile, because Manny knew that his craft's radar signature wasn't much bigger than a fat seagull's. It was a stupid move by an undertrained *molodoy;* an action for which he'd probably be punished above and beyond standard new-recruit hazing. Any soldier with a decent amount of training would have ignored that faint blip on the tracking radar.

What the goddamn, suffering *molodoy* would never know was that he'd actually done his job exactly right.

Once on Manny's tail, there was only so much that could be done to disguise the thousand degrees of heat exhaust from his turbine engine. The missile had flown close enough to sniff out that heat signature and zeroed in. It moved at almost Mach 2 and he moved at about one-tenth of that.

A locked-on *Igla* wasn't something that

was evaded by a quick maneuver. The "needle" as it was aptly named, was about to drill his ass. It ignored the signal-blocking chaff that Manny dispersed. Firing off a round of distracting flares would illuminate and pinpoint his location for much more substantial forces. He saw only one chance and punched for it. Head for the sea.

The high cliffs south of Sevastopol were just close enough for him to dive over the edge and buy himself a few seconds before the missile reacquired. A half kilometer out from shore, he stalled the helicopter hard, heaving back on the cyclic until the joystick was jammed into his gut. His Little Bird groaned and wept, but it slammed from a hundred and seventy-five miles an hour to under forty in moments.

He armed the self-destruct charges, then unsnapped his belt, and dove out the doorway.

He was less than halfway to the water when the Igla caught up with his Little Bird. The explosion was blinding in its reflection off the water, the concussive punch of combined missile and destruct charges made the last twenty-five feet of his fall go by very quickly.

2

It felt as if Alisa had been undercover her entire life. First from the ruling government of the Prime Minister turned dictator and now from the Russians. Their recent annexation of Crimea had made her job a hundred times more dangerous and she stayed because she didn't know what else to do. She was trapped between the Russian SVR, their version of the CIA, who would ruin her day if her role was ever discovered, and the CIA itself with their promises of safe passage out…if she could just hold on a while longer and find out about whatever was next on their never-ending list.

Then Sergey of the SVR had taken a sudden interest in her, more than just trying to bed her. He began dropping by her desk at work, or just happening to run into her when she was out at a club.

Knowing she'd reached her limit, she'd finally convinced the CIA that it was time to honor their commitment and send in an extraction team as she had no way of escaping on her own.

For twenty hours she'd cowered in fear, dodging shadows and afraid at each moment that she'd be taken into custody and never see daylight again. Just as she was preparing to leave and work her slow way to the extraction rendezvous—a journey that would take half the night—a knock had sounded on her door.

Instead a phalanx of guards, there had been only Sergey. He had offered to "protect" her in exchange for certain "services." She didn't need to watch where his eyes remained fixed to know what services he was interested in and didn't care to guess how brief a respite from prison his protection would offer should she consent.

Then Sergey had made the mistake—fatal

as it turned out—of tapping his briefcase and saying he had a report he would turn in if she did not agree.

She had read the report while Sergey quietly sank to the bottom of Pivdenna Bay. He had gotten only a few facts right, but two of them were completely damning—they also told her who among her informants must be a double agent for the SVR, as that part of the report was too accurate. When she found the thumb drive in his pants pocket, with a copy of the report on it, she decided that Sergey was definitely arrogant enough to have left no form of "Open this file if I do not return" at the office.

Just in case, Alisa would have to die tonight along with the ever-so-surprised Sergey. Irina (still a top-twenty name among Ukrainian women) would be born tomorrow with fresh papers and a new address. She had deep connections in both the "renegade terrorist" Ukrainian camp and the Russian "our special forces Spetsnaz aren't really here" camp (to which Sergey had belonged).

If Sergey had truly kept everything to himself, then there was only one person who still could expose her, Lesia Melnyk. Lesia was General Vlad Kozlov's mistress and worked in the same department as Alisa. She had been Alisa's first friend in a long time and the betrayal cut deep.

Alisa decided that except for Lesia she was safe enough. Her thinking was that with Sergey's demise and his report gone, an identity change should be enough to protect her. She could stay and continue running her other contacts, so she called off the extraction.

The other reason to stay was unprofessional as hell and she didn't care. Lesia was her supposed best friend and the first person she'd turned, or thought she had. Alisa wanted revenge—badly.

Alisa put the thumb drive in her pocket. A glance around the apartment hurt so much. She wanted to take everything and could take nothing. She slipped her parents' photo in her pocket, tossed the paper copy of Sergey's report along with a couple recent copies of *Pravda* on top of her stove, set the burners on high, and left quickly.

By the time she had walked a block away, her one-bedroom kvartira (rather than kvar*tyra* as

Sevastopol was no longer a Ukrainian city but rather a Russian one) was on fire. When she glanced back two blocks later, it was engulfed and flames were streaming out the windows. She wore a dead man's clothes, which weren't a bad fit except for being very tight across the chest even without a bra (it would have helped if Sergey had worked out more in life), and had her long blond hair tucked up into a worker's cap. The May weather was too warm for a *ushanka* fur hat. She'd liked that hat and hated to leave it behind in the flames.

For three nameless hours, she slouched her way across the city and back. No longer Alisa and not yet Irina, she watched carefully for a tail.

After that she sat for an hour in the back of Zeppelin Club. It was Friday night and the workweek crowd was blowing out as desperately as they could. The loud Euro pop was predictably awful though the "exotic" female dancers managed to not look too bored. Her stool at a small table along the far side of the stage allowed her to watch the entrance between the dancers' bare legs and other body parts as they arched and writhed. It was hard to believe, but perhaps Sergey really had been dumb enough to confront a foreign agent without a backup.

She spent another hour drinking at a shadowed table in a porn club, the favorite of one of her contacts, but gave up around four a.m. while the party was still rolling hard (pun intended). She staggered her way back past Alisa's apartment. The fire brigade had been and gone. The burned shell would reveal nothing that would arouse suspicions except for its no-longer-existent renter's failure to return. No one waited in the shadows looking for a woman with long blond hair and serious curves. And certainly not for a drunken man staggering homeward.

She hadn't meant to drink as much as she did, though it was the leading national pastime. That, and griping about the brutal Russians or the lazy Ukrainians—depending on who you were drinking with: the noble Ukrainians or the world-conquering Russians. But the nerves had gotten to her. She'd made it through the Russian invasion of Crimea more calmly than facing exposure by Sergey. Had he been just one tiny bit less interested in her breasts, she'd probably be screaming in an SVR torture cell at the moment.

And if she'd been one bit less angry at Lesia Melnyk, she'd have climbed on the damned helicopter and been safe by now. But the anger had grown rather than abating. The alcohol buffered none of the emotions ripping at her.

She leaned her head against the door of the safe house, just three streets over from her burned-out apartment, and struggled to catch her breath. Her hands were shaky as she reached for her keys.

Purse, where was her purse?

No, dressed as a man now.

Pants pocket.

Key in door, the soft click of the lock.

And at the same moment there was a soft sound behind her, then a jabbing pressure in the middle of her back.

"*Medlenno*," a voice commanded in Russian. Slowly indeed.

3

Manny eased through the doorway and kept his Glock 19 pressed against the man's back until they were both inside. He'd been through far too much shit in the last ten hours to trust anyone, safe house or not.

Impossibly, he hadn't died despite his helicopter being shot down by a missile. However, the explosion had happened less than a thousand meters from a Russian frigate, so there was no way for Quinn and Patty in the backup helo to fish his ass out of the water without being targeted themselves.

The Russians had been slow to arrive and

inspect the explosion area, which had allowed him time to swim to shore unobserved. Then the CIA had tried stonewalling on the location of their safe house. That had given him his first smile as he hid at the base of a Crimean cliff, carefully covered in sand except for his face despite the nighttime darkness. He wouldn't want to be one of Langley's CIA headquarters personnel right now, not with his 5E commanders Pete Napier and Daniella Delacroix after them. They'd coughed up the safe house address eventually.

Manny had made selections from a couple of clotheslines and then simply walked across the city. Sometimes brash paid off. No one stopped him, except for his nerves which had attempted to asphyxiate him at every step. When he'd arrived, the door was locked. He really hated Crimea.

The CIA's passive-aggressive goddamn joke, not telling him where to find the key. If he ever met the bastard who—

Unproductive thinking!

The ground floor was totally locked and barred.

He'd climbed up to a small balcony, that

was equally fortified, and squatted down while he tried to figure out what to do. The traffic was light in this neighborhood at oh-four-bumfuck in the morning, just some drunk weaving his lazy ass home.

Then the drunk had stepped up to the safe house door directly below Manny's balcony. He waited until the man almost had the door open, then dropped down and crowded him inside.

Once through the door, he shoved the drunk up against the wall. If this was the caliber of men the CIA could find, it was no wonder the Russians had moved in so easily.

The house was quiet and dark. The very first light of dawn filtered weakly through a small window set above the door, just enough to see shapes.

Without moving his weapon, Manny kicked the man's feet apart and forced him to raise his hands, palm-flat, against the wall. Then he began checking out the man. A vicious flick-blade in his sock. Manny almost missed the thin strap for the hideaway holster inside his thigh—for hidden carry but not quick draw, he'd pants the guy in a moment and take it. Then he reached to check the crotch, but there was nothing there.

The drunk began cursing in slurred Russian, but he nudged his sidearm hard against his kidney…no, her kidney…and the Russian grunted and began complaining louder.

"Zatknis!"

The drunk woman continued to grumble, but she did so more quietly. He reached around to undo her belt and pants enough to recover the hidden weapon. Her jacket gave up nothing except a thumb drive which he pocketed. Then he yanked the jacket off her and tossed it aside just in case he'd missed something. Another blade, this time tucked down between ample breasts, and a shower of long hair when he knocked the cap aside. He couldn't feel anything inside the cap except a photo that it was too dark to see.

He eased away until he was well out of reach with his back against the front door so that there would be no surprises. Then he flicked on a light on a small table.

"Turn. Slowly," he said in Russian.

"Your accent. It is terrible," the woman

mumbled in heavily-inflected English as she turned.

"So sue me."

She rolled over, still leaning against the wall for support, until her back was pressed against it. Without the jacket, her men's clothing didn't mask a thing about her. Trim, built, long blond hair that cascaded past her shoulders, and piercing blue eyes in a lovely face.

"Damn. I can see I should have visited Crimea sooner."

"Go and take yourself to hells, Yankee. Who are you?"

"Prince Charming. And it's 'to hell' but you're too late, I'm already there. Who are you?"

"I do not know this anymore," her voice wavered. "Call me the Grand Duchess Anastasia for all I care," then the woman slid down the wall to sit on her butt. "Nothing left but ashes." She rubbed at her face then leaned her head back against the plaster. Her hands dropped into her lap.

Manny felt as exhausted as she looked. He'd been running mostly on adrenalin since they'd woken him at this time yesterday morning, a thousand kilometers away.

Her head tipped slightly to one side.
Then she softly began to snore.
Manny really, really hated Crimea.

4

Alisa woke slowly.

Except she wasn't Alisa anymore. She was… Irina now. Irina. Had to repeat her new name until it was second nature. Irina Kovalenko. Irina Kovalenko.

Irina remembered her apartment burning, no, her torching her own apartment. She remembered…

Chyort voz'mi! She remembered slitting Sergey's throat. She'd managed to lead him down to an out-of-the-way dock along the waterfront after convincing him that taking her out to dinner was a sure path to success with her—thankfully Sevastopol was mostly waterfront. And while he'd been enjoying himself, groping her breasts with brutal strength, she'd slipped a blade up through the soft underpart of his chin and managed to cut his brainstem just like in training. For a moment he'd squeezed her breasts so convulsively hard that she was the one who almost cried out. Then he let go and slumped to the planking. She'd stripped him, tied an anchor that she stole from one of the boats about his ankles, and quietly disposed of the first person she'd ever killed.

But she'd held it together, by god. She'd made it back to her apartment, studied his report, made a plan, and executed her escape.

She made good until…the man at the door. He'd come out of nowhere. She'd had no tail; she was certain of it.

And then there'd been a gun at her back.

An American man who—

Irina tried to sit up—and flopped back on the mattress. Now that she'd tried to move, she could feel the ropes about her wrist and ankles. Not tight but, she pulled on them, not giving either.

"*Der'mo!*" She opened her eyes. *Oh shit!*

She was in a small, dingy bedroom. A battered dresser. A small, dust-hazed mirror. The ugliest wallpaper on the planet, blue with large red roses, that was peeling at the corners.

And a bed, the one she was tied to. Her wrists were above her head, not uncomfortably so, but too far to reach the knots with her teeth. Her ankles were tied, but she could still feel her toes, so the circulation wasn't cut off. A slight motion and she could tell that she still wore a shirt and her panties, but none of her weapons. A blanket lay over her, a woolen one. It itched.

If this was an SVR prison cell, it was much more luxurious than she'd expected. If this was a hotel…it sucked!

She raised her head to look about more carefully. Beyond the foot of the bed a man slumped deep in a battered armchair. He was slender, with dark hair that needed a trim. He needed a shave as well. His sidearm was on his lap, his booted feet were crossed on the foot of her bed, and his dark eyes were watching her.

"Bet you feel like shit," his voice was low and painfully astute.

Her hangover sprang to the foreground. "*Spasibo, parshiviy.* I had not noticed."

"You're welcome and I'm only an asshole when I'm in the mood. At the moment, I'm totally there. You know, it's not your average person who falls asleep at gunpoint."

"Long day," she countered.

"Tell me about it."

She closed her eyes and swore to herself that she'd never drink vodka again.

"Seriously, tell me about it. Start with your name."

"My name is Irina," Irina what? Started with a K. "Irina Kovalenko." Her gaff shouldn't be too noticeable. "Had too much to drink."

"That explains the night, now tell me about the day."

She opened her eyes long enough to glare at him. A light curtain across the window kept her from telling what time of day it was, though it was still bright enough to hurt. She closed her eyes and let her head drop back to the pillow again.

"Who are *you, tolstak?*" Because she wasn't about to tell some unknown fat-ass about her day.

5

Interesting place you have here, Grand Duchess." Manny made it conversational when it became clear she wasn't going to say anything more.

She looked at him strangely when he called her that. Too far gone last night to remember naming herself as the youngest of the old Czar's children.

Once he'd been sure that she wasn't feigning sleep, he'd stripped her outer clothes, tied her to the bed, and tucked her in. Then he'd investigated the house.

The interior dimensions hadn't matched

the exterior and it hadn't taken him long to figure out why. First and second floor each had hidden rooms, subtle ones, not easy to notice. Except he'd been trained by the very best instructors the US Army had on room clearing techniques—including identifying and opening hidden spaces. One space was packed with clothing in multiple sexes and sizes. He selected a few pieces that fit better than what he'd been able to scavenge off the clothesline. The other space had weapons, a nice forgery setup for making false passports, and a few radios.

He'd also found a laptop and checked out the thumb drive he'd taken from her pocket. If she'd done even half of what was in the report he found there, he was impressed as hell. But it didn't mean that he trusted her either.

"Not my place," the blond mumbled without opening her eyes. Christ, he could look at her all day. Even hungover she was a knockout. While crossing the city last night he'd noted that Ukrainian women were on the whole exceptionally attractive, but she was above and beyond.

"No. It's the CIA's I assume, since they sent me here. And yet you had a key. What's a drunken trollop doing with a key to a CIA safe house?"

"I am no a drunken trollop!" She was angry enough to ignore her hangover and glare at him, at least one eye's worth.

He took pity on her and reached over to close one of the heavier curtains.

"What is trollop?" She asked in a much gentler tone.

"Whatever you say, Duchess. You were skunk-drunk last night, and parading around in men's clothes without a bra despite your impressive figure. Now who the hell *are* you?" He'd had enough of stupid games. "And try to come up with a real name this time."

She sighed. "If I do, will you get me some aspirin?"

"Sure. Might even let you take it too, Duchess."

"You would make lousy interrogator for SVR. No call me that."

"Whatever you say, Duchess. But I'm one hell of a pilot."

That brought her head back up to look at him, "Pilot for the Americans? The Night Stalkers?"

He started to nod and then could only think of one way she could know that. It jolted him to his feet clenching his weapon.

She cringed, so he slammed the pistol into his belt. He'd left his holster in the back of a handy police cruiser last night—which was bound to confuse the crap out of them though it had no markings on it.

"You bitch!" She flinched as if he'd struck her. He'd never hit a woman, but he was awfully tempted to strangle one at the moment. "You cancelled an extract less than sixty seconds from pickup?"

"No! I call three hours before. Three hours!"

Manny didn't even know how to answer that.

It eventually led him to his untying her and the two of them sitting across the kitchen table from each other. It had one leg too short and kept rocking back and forth as they both drank burned coffee made with ancient grounds. The kitchen was as disreputable as the table and the only food was a bag of rice that probably had been there since before the Soviet Union had imploded.

They determined that their watches were in sync. The abort-mission command had taken three hours (minus sixty seconds) to worm its way out of Langley and out to the field. Insane. Manny knew the Night Stalkers wouldn't have delayed such a message; they'd know the risk.

"Goddamn spooks," he couldn't help complaining.

"Spooks? Ah, spies. I too am spy, but I am agreeing very much."

He smiled. It was hard not to smile at her. And not just because of her physical attributes. He enjoyed her in-your-face personality—milquetoast, quiet women never did it for him and she was anything but. Plus, he certainly did like the way she looked in just a men's shirt, underwear, and socks. If she thought she was playing him by not getting fully dressed, it wasn't going to work—but he wasn't going to file any complaints about the scenery. For some reason the plain white socks just made the whole outfit real damn cute.

She rested her elbows on the grimy table and leaned her head down into her hands. Her shirt hung forward and the scenery got a whole lot better. The upper part of her breasts were full, creamy…and bore dark patches the size of fingerprints.

"Who marked you, Grand Duchess?"

"I tell you to stop—" She glanced up at him, noticed the direction of his attention, then scowled before looking down at her own chest. "*Moodak!* That bloody dead bastard!"

And she told him about the unlamented Sergey and the burned-out apartment.

"If your cover was gone, why the hell did you cancel the extract?"

"You supposed to save me, but you shot from sky?" She teased him. "Not the kind of hero-pilot a good girl is looking for."

"Then what kind of hero-pilot is 'a good girl' looking for?"

6

This girl was enjoying the hero-pilot sitting just across from her. He kept surprising her. Soon she might be telling him her real story. Actually, probably no reason not to. Why not.

"I am Lyudmila Bykov. That is truth. I'm am named for Lyudmila the most famous woman sniper ever. She kill many German and Romanians here, in Sevastopol, during the World War Second. I am also pissed-off war orphan. Pissed-off, yes?"

Manny nodded that she'd gotten it right.

"I am nineteen when the Prime Minister Yanukovych enforcers put down the supporters of opposition leader Yulia Tymoshenko. Yulia want closer ties to NATO and was jailed for it. Everybody except Russia declare her trial all bad. Unfair. My parents were very close to Yulia and were executed in their beds by 'criminals unknown.' A CIA recruiter found me when I was very drunk and very, very pissed-off. With their help I change my name, I start working here as coordinator, to help in government offices, with Russian Black Sea Fleet. You know they are stationed here? In Sevastopol?"

"I almost got to see them up close and personal last night," and she didn't like the darkness of the frown on his face. Ever since he had untied her, he had looked relaxed and cheerful. But she did not forget the gun that was still sticking out from his belt and she could see the anger still there. She was glad it was not aimed at her.

"I still work in office. No, no more. Last night I killed Alisa and became Irinia."

"Who is really Lyudmila. Good story, Grand Duchess."

"Why do you keep calling me this?"

Manny shrugged as he crossed to the stove.

His movements were quick and precise. It was the third time he had freshened their coffees though neither of them were drinking much. She had the feeling that he wasn't very good at sitting still. Usually she wasn't either, but the aspirin hadn't gone to her head.

"Where did you learn such good English?"

"Parents. They buy me tutor so I'm ready to ready to serve in Tymoshenko's government. As I say, true believers for all the no good it did them."

"So how to get out of here?" Manny was pacing about the kitchen.

"Out of where?"

"Crimea."

She looked up at him, "I'm not leaving."

"You don't *look* stupid."

"There's someone who betrayed me. I have to deal with that." She was going to take Lesia Melnyk apart if it was the last thing she did to that *sooka!*

"You going to end up dead in the process?"

She didn't have a good answer to that.

This time Manny came to a stop. He squatted close in front of her. "There's got to be a better choice than staying for revenge, Lyudmila."

If there was, she couldn't think of it. Hope was something she had stopped believing in long before Sergey and his report.

"My parents called me Mila," and she did her best not to cry. Perhaps she would see them soon…too bad she didn't believe in that either.

7

It rapidly became clear to Manny that he wasn't going to make it out of Sevastopol alive without Mila's help. She made a few discreet inquiries among her friends and Russian security was way up since the destruction of his helicopter. Nobody knew what had exploded outside their harbor, but their increased readiness eliminated any rescue by air. And by sea was even dodgier, which was why they'd risked the extraction by air in the first place.

"Sometimes the only way out is through," he had to solve this.

For two days they barely slept as they

strategized, discarding theories and escape routes as fast as they thought them up.

"There's no way that cutting your hair and dying it black would buy you more than a few days. It didn't work in the Jason Bourne movies. It won't work for you, Duchess. You're too goddamn beautiful. And if you don't show up for work on Monday, all sorts of alarms will going off."

After the initial sadness that had almost broken his heart to watch, Mila rallied. Her knowledge of government and the Russian military was deep…and not helping.

"Maybe our ticket out of here is the woman who betrayed you. Tell me about your traitor"—weird thing to say to a spy. "This Lesia who informed on you to the SVR. We have to figure this out."

When he said "we" she'd shot him a smile that could have lit up the sky.

"What?"

"For almost a decade it has been 'me,'" her voice was an intimate whisper. "You said 'we.'"

"That's how the world spins," he spoke quickly to cover what he really wanted to do next.

He crossed to the window to get a little more distance.

"I've got a team out there working the problem for me," he waved toward the back of the building next door, an abandoned warehouse.

His team had fed him several ideas during very brief radio calls, though none had panned out yet.

"The whole world doesn't work like the Russians and the CIA. Hell, I thought Patty and Quinn were going to fly right into the Russians' guns to extract me. I had to risk the radio to call them off while I was swimming for shore."

And when he was sure that he once again had control of himself, they went back to their planning, but it had changed. It had changed from 'me' to 'we' in a way that Manny hadn't anticipated. High pressure situation be damned, every single thing he learned about Grand Duchess Lyudmila of Sevastopol, the more he appreciated her. At a level of risk that only a Night Stalker could understand, she had fed a constant stream of actionable intelligence to the West. It hadn't been enough to save Crimea from the Russians, but it had probably saved the rest of the country from invasion.

By Sunday night they had a plan.

It was shaky as hell, but they had one.

When they were both too weary to think up another contingency, they'd dropped down side by side on a couch in what could laughably be called a living room.

"What do you think our chances are? To survival?"

Manny shrugged, "Anyone else, thirty percent at best. You and me, Duchess? I'm betting my life on it being a hundred."

"Are you always so positive?"

"Never saw much fun in focusing on the other side of that coin. I mess up plenty, but that's not where I live."

"That is good," she nodded to herself, then nodded again. Her hair a slick slide of gold that he wanted to toy with every time she moved. "It's not what I have done in past, but it's what I will do in future. What about after?"

"You mean after, as in if we get out of this alive?"

8

She poked him in the ribs, "*When* we get out of this alive." She liked the intimacy of the gesture.

"Right. Well, I've got some buddies who would love to meet you."

Mila could feel her skin go cold. She knew what kind of "buddies" people wanted to introduce pretty blonds to. It had served her well as a spy in the Ukraine, but Alisa, Irina, and Lyudmila were all three sick of being used for their body.

"They're in this odd little intelligence group with no name. Finding a trained insider in Ukrainian politics, fluent in English and Russian…they're definitely going to want to meet you."

"That…" wasn't what she'd been expecting. "Do they work with you very much?" Or would he be far away if she worked with them?

Manny was nodding. "That's kind of their purpose. It would be nice if…"

She could hear him taper off, as if worried that he'd crossed some line. He was the strangest man she'd ever met.

First, she hadn't woken up naked and raped.

Once he'd released her—which he had done long before she would have if their roles had been reversed—she'd waited through the first day, expecting it to happen anyway. Or at least sex to happen; he didn't strike her as a cruel man.

But by now, they'd rarely been more than a step apart for two days and still he'd done nothing, though the way he watched her there was no question he'd wanted to.

Well, now she wanted to as well. No matter what he said, their chances weren't good—their plan was simply the best of many terrible options.

She rose and, taking him by the hand, pulled him to his feet. Once they reached the bedroom, he did an incredible job of making her feel absolutely grand.

9

"Hi, honey. Look who else decided to come along with Lesia?"

Manny just about swallowed his tongue. Their plan had included a dinner with the woman who had betrayed Mila's—no, she was back to being Alisa for one more night—Alisa's trust.

Just her.

Instead, the two women were followed closely by a man in full military uniform who wore the one star and no red stripes insignia of a major general of the Russian Federation.

"This is Lesia. Who I told you so much

about," Alisa was being a bubbly blond that he barely recognized, the party-girl facade worn by the Grand Duchess of sheer balls—bringing a major general to dinner. She turned to her former friend, a very attractive brunette. "And this is Manny. Isn't he just the cutest?"

That was a new one, but Manny wasn't going to argue.

Their escape plan was to convince Lesia to invite them out to her dacha in the country… where she apparently played mistress with her lover the general. Once clear of Sevastopol and the heavy protection surrounding the Black Sea Fleet, they could signal Patty and Quinn to meet them at the dacha, backed up by the hammer blow of the 5E Company in close support.

However, Lesia had not come alone.

"And this is Vlad," the crazy blond hung onto the general's arm for a moment. "He's in charge of the Naval helicopter fleet at Kacha." Alisa said that last bit like it was a slightly confusing throwaway line, but Manny heard "helicopter fleet" loud and clear. In that moment he forgave Alisa everything. There had to be a way to use this.

He was suddenly damn glad that he'd arranged for the fliers of the 5E to hold at thirty kilometers out, pending his final call. He wanted to avoid a reenactment of three nights ago and it was a distance they could cover in six minutes or less. Who could predict where the evening was headed.

Dinner was a strange and surreal affair. Manny's role was pretending to be a foreign correspondent, a Canadian who had somehow finagled a visa into an area where no press were allowed. Except he knew nothing about being a reporter and his one trip to Canada had been a drunk weekend during the Stanley Cup hockey playoffs between the New York Rangers and the Montréal Canadiens.

The bait they'd dangled to get Lesia to the meal had been vague hints that Manny was only posing as a Canadian reporter and was actually Alisa's "big" contact. A next-tier intelligence coup that Lesia would be unable to resist. So unable to resist, that she'd brought the general along to witness her glory. Perhaps if she delivered both US agents, the unmentioned wife would become powerless and the beautiful Lesia would gain the Mrs. General prize.

Throughout the meal, Alisa teased and flirted outrageously. Rather than playing footsie under the table, as would fit the events going on above the table, she kept a constant hard pressure of her leg wrapped about his. He could tell her nerves were stretched right near the breaking point, almost as badly as the woman he'd met three days ago—drunk and dressed as a man.

But rather than showing it, she was magnificent. Sparkling, downright effervescent, and damned fun despite the crazy situation.

Not surprisingly, the dinner topic that he and Vlad landed on was helicopters. As long as that was the topic, Manny could pretend to be a war correspondent who knew about helicopters from various embeds he'd done with forward teams.

It took a while for Manny to realize that Vlad was out of the loop here. He was just under the impression that he was having a lively dinner with one of his mistress' friends. And he definitely liked Alisa. So much so that Manny was forced to pay more and more attention to the mistress so that she didn't become angry.

Then Alisa let slip that Manny had flown helicopters himself.

Military ones.

What the hell? He didn't catch on to what she could possibly be thinking until she nodded ever so slightly toward the general, at the same moment she kicked him sharply under the table.

After that the conversation shifted. He and General Vlad Kozlov were suddenly best buddies and soon Manny was dancing around the edges of what technologic insights he could share without violating his own Top Secret clearance.

And Lesia was, in his amateur-reporter opinion, no master spy. However, she was a very drunk one and was soon swept up in the chatter of their lively evening.

10

Alisa hung on for the wild and drunken ride to Kacha Airbase. It turned out that nothing would do, after a little coaxing and a few teasing suggestions on her own part, except for General Vlad Kozlov to show Manny the latest technology out of Russia. It had just arrived and he was very proud of having it under his local command.

"I am only Ukrainian general that Russians keep," he'd boasted. "They trust me very much. I am most important Ukrainian man in Crimea military."

Thankfully being a major general also

earned him a driver, a silent and sober man able to escort them safely across the twenty-kilometer transit from the restaurant in the heart of Sevastopol to the base. The general was certainly in no condition to drive. He and Manny were singing together in some terrible mixture of three languages.

"It is beautiful machine. It will make Americans sick it so good," the general slipped back and forth between Ukrainian and Russian making his speech broken and slurred. Lesia was even worse off.

Alisa—she had to stay solidly in her Alisa mode just a while longer—wished she could drag Manny aside. First, she'd kiss him for being so completely amazing at dinner.

Truth be told, she couldn't wait to jump him. She'd been scared to death, but Manny had been so calm and smooth that everything had worked…so far.

That was the second thing she wanted to do: drag Manny aside and ask, "What the hell are we doing?" Any remnants of their original plan had been cleared off the table along with the *tabak börek* dumplings with broth and long before the arrival of the *pennik* apricot pie and the third bottle of Massandra wine—served with lots of vodka on the side.

Of course Manny was too sotted to answer. More than once he'd groped Lesia's breast instead of her own. It was ironic, considering how they'd met, that she was the only one still sober enough to care about such things.

But before she could collect her thoughts more than to recognize that the hand on her knee and working its way up her skirt was not Manny's, they arrived at the airbase.

Reacting to steadfast refusal on Manny's part, the general soon forced him into the pilot's seat then sat beside him in the copilot's seat. She and Lesia were placed close behind them at the engineering stations.

"This," Vlad slapped the top of the central console. "This is a Kamov Ka-35 Airborne Early Warning platform. With this, we can see ballistic missile, submarine launch, ship launch, American helicopter…" He nudged Manny with an elbow and apparently thought he was lowering his voice, though he wasn't. "We can even see what our women would hide from us but is there for a man's taking. *Da? Da?*"

"Yes!" Manny agreed with a fist pump.

The general tried to copy the gesture but was so drunk that he cracked his elbow hard on the door. Lesia had passed out in her seat.

"Should we take it up for a test?" Manny asked in an oddly meek tone, then he turned and winked at her—very soberly.

Take it up for a... Oh my god! Manny was brilliant. The newest Russian technology could take them out of Crimea…and it would be a major coup to deliver it to the American technicians for study. There wouldn't even be any political fallout as it would look like the general and his mistress were defecting. If this worked, the Americans would also get everything Lesia and Vlad knew.

Manny winked again and nodded toward the general.

Oh!

"Please, Vlad," Alisa poured all the begging she could into her voice. She leaned forward between the pilots' seats far enough to press a breast against his arm and pawed at his chest. "Please, Vlad. Let me see her fly!"

"*Zroby tse!*" The general commanded with a broad wave of his arm that clipped Manny with a solid punch. "Do it! *Da,* go!" Then he shouted confidentially to Manny, "We shall show both these wenches many fine things tonight."

And Manny began cycling up the helicopter. As soon as the radios blinked to life, he spoke to the general.

"You better tell the tower we're taking it out. So they don't shoot us down." He said it like the funniest joke in the world and Vlad roared with laughter.

"Yes! Yes! Good idea!"

Then Alisa had another idea and once more held tightly onto the general's arm, "Take us over the water. I want to see the moonlight on the Black Sea. It's *so* romantic, Vlad. Tell them that, too."

And the general did.

11

"This is Lieutenant Manfred Malcolm. Are we a go?"

"Roger that," the Air Mission Commander called out. "We're a go."

"This should be a quick one, if we can trust intel," Manny called back, knowing exactly who had done the background research for the mission.

"Damn straight you can, Mr. Lieutenant Manny!" Mila's tone was teasing as she cut into the radio circuit. Her language had become as rough as his own. It sounded good on her, brash and full of life.

He *knew* he could trust her. Over the last six months she'd proven herself every bit as sharp as she was beautiful.

"And you make it quick. No three-day holiday in Crimea this time. We have wedding tomorrow. I may be single woman going up this aisle, but I will be married woman walking back down this aisle. That, or you will not be walking so good. *Da?*"

"Whatever you say, Duchess." He yanked up on the collective and shoved the cyclic forward to lay the hammer down hard. "On my way."

About the Author

M. L. Buchman has over 50 novels and 30 short stories in print. His military romantic suspense books have been named Barnes & Noble and NPR "Top 5 of the year" and twice *Booklist* "Top 10 of the Year," placing two titles on their "Top 101 Romances of the Last 10 Years" list. He has been nominated for the Reviewer's Choice Award for "Top 10 Romantic Suspense of the Year" by *RT Book Reviews* and was a 2016 RWA RITA finalist. In addition to romance, he also writes thrillers, fantasy, and science fiction.

In among his career as a corporate project

manager he has: rebuilt and single-handed a fifty-foot sailboat, both flown and jumped out of airplanes, designed and built two houses, and bicycled solo around the world.

He is now making his living as a full-time writer on the Oregon Coast with his beloved wife. He is constantly amazed at what you can do with a degree in Geophysics. You may keep up with his writing by subscribing to his newsletter at www.mlbuchman.com.

If you enjoyed this story, you might also enjoy:

Target of the Heart (excerpt)
-a Night Stalkers 5E novel-

Major Pete Napier hovered his MH-47G Chinook helicopter ten kilometers outside of Lhasa, Tibet and a mere two inches off the tundra. A mixed action team of Delta Force and The Activity—the slipperiest intel group on the planet—flung themselves aboard.

The additional load sent an infinitesimal shift in the cyclic control in his right hand. The hydraulics to close the rear loading ramp hummed through the entire frame of the massive helicopter. By the time his crew chief could reach forward to slap an "all secure" signal against his shoulder, they were already ten feet up and fifty out. That was enough altitude. He kept the nose down as he clawed for speed in the thin air at eleven thousand feet.

"Totally worth it," one of the D-boys announced as soon as he was on the Chinook's internal intercom.

He'd have to remember to tell that to the two Black Hawks flying guard for him…when they were in a friendly country and could risk a radio transmission. This deep inside China—or rather Chinese-held territory as the CIA's mission-briefing spook had insisted on calling it—radios attracted attention and were only used to avoid imminent death and destruction.

"Great, now I just need to get us out of this alive."

"Do that, Pete. We'd appreciate it."

He wished to hell he had a stealth bird like the one that had gone into bin Laden's compound. But the one that had crashed during that raid had been blown up. Where there was one, there were always two, but the second had gone back into hiding as thoroughly as if it had never existed. He hadn't heard a word about it since.

The Tibetan terrain was amazing, even if all he could see of it was the monochromatic green of night vision. And blackness. The largest city in Tibet lay a mere ten kilometers away and they were flying over barren wilderness. He could crash out here and no one would know for decades unless some yak herder stumbled upon them. Or were yaks in Mongolia? He was a corn-fed, white boy from Colorado, what did he know about Tibet? Most of the countries he'd flown into on black ops missions he'd only seen at night anyway.

While moving very, very fast.

Like now.

The inside of his visor was painted with overlapping readouts. A pre-defined terrain map, the best that modern satellite imaging could build made the first layer. This wasn't some crappy, on-line, look-at-a-picture-of-your-house display. Someone had a pile of dung outside their goat pen? He could see it, tell you how high it was, and probably say if they were pygmy goats or full-size LaManchas by the size of their shit-pellets if he zoomed in.

On top of that were projected the forward-looking infrared camera images. The FLIR imaging gave him a real-time overlay, in case someone had put an addition onto their goat shed since the last satellite pass, or parked their tractor across his intended flight path.

His nervous system was paying autonomic attention to that combined landscape. He also compensated for the thin air at altitude as he instinctively chose when to start his climb over said goat shed or his swerve around it.

It was the third layer, the tactical display that had most of his attention. At least he and the two Black Hawks flying escort on him were finally on the move.

To insert this deep into Tibet, without passing over Bhutan or Nepal, they'd had to add wingtanks on the Black Hawks' hardpoints where he'd much rather have a couple banks of

Hellfire missiles. Still, they had 20mm chain guns and the crew chiefs had miniguns which was some comfort.

While the action team was busy infiltrating the capital city and gathering intelligence on the particularly brutal Chinese assistant administrator, he and his crews had been squatting out in the wilderness under a camouflage net designed to make his helo look like just another god-forsaken Himalayan lump of granite.

Command had determined that it was better for the helos to wait on site through the day than risk flying out and back in. He and his crew had stood shifts on guard duty, but none of them had slept. They'd been flying together too long to have any new jokes, so they'd played a lot of cribbage. He'd long ago ruled no gambling on a mission, after a fistfight had broken out about a bluff hand that cost a Marine three hundred and forty-seven dollars. Marines hated losing to Army no matter how many times it happened. They'd had to sit on him for a long time before he calmed down.

Tonight's mission was part of an on-going campaign to discredit the Chinese "presence"

Target of the Heart (excerpt)

in Tibet on the international stage—as if occupying the country the last sixty years didn't count toward ruling, whether invited or not. As usual, there was a crucial vote coming up at the U.N.—that, as usual, the Chinese could be guaranteed to ignore. However, the ever-hopeful CIA was in a hurry to make sure that any damaging information that they could validate was disseminated as thoroughly as possible prior to the vote.

Not his concern.

His concern was, were they going to pass over some Chinese sentry post at their top speed of a hundred and ninety-six miles an hour? The sentries would then call down a couple Shenyang J-16 jet fighters that could hustle along at Mach 2 to fry his sorry ass. He knew there was a pair of them parked at Lhasa along with some older gear that would be just as effective against his three helos.

"Don't suppose you could get a move on, Pete?"

"Eat shit, Nicolai!" He was a good man to have as a copilot. Pete knew he was holding on too tight, and Nicolai knew that a joke was the right way to ease the moment.

He, Nicolai, and the four pilots in the two Black Hawks had a long way to go tonight and he'd never make it if he stayed so tight on the controls that he could barely maneuver. Pete eased off and felt his fingers tingle with the rush of returning blood. They dove down into gorges and followed them as long as they dared. They hugged cliff walls at every opportunity to decrease their radar profile. And they climbed.

That was the true danger—they would be up near the helos' limits when they crossed over the backbone of the Himalayas in their rush for India. The air was so rarefied that they burned fuel at a prodigious rate. Their reserve didn't allow for any extended battles while crossing the border…not for any battle at all really.

# # #

It was pitch dark outside her helicopter when Captain Danielle Delacroix stamped on the left rudder pedal while giving the big Chinook right-directed control on the cyclic. It tipped her most of the way onto her side, but let her continue in a straight line. A Chinook's rotors were sixty feet across—front to back they overlapped to make the spread a hundred feet long. By cross-controlling her bird to tip it, she managed to execute a straight line between two mock pylons only thirty feet apart. They were made of thin cloth so they wouldn't down the helo if you sliced one—she was the only trainee to not have cut one yet.

At her current angle of attack, she took up less than a half-rotor of width, just twenty-four feet. That left her nearly three feet to either side, sufficient as she was moving at under a hundred knots.

The training instructor sitting beside her in the copilot's seat didn't react as she swooped through the training course at Fort Campbell, Kentucky. Only child of a single mother, she was used to providing her own feedback loops, so she didn't expect anything else. Those who expected outside validation rarely survived the SOAR induction testing, never mind the two years of training that followed.

As a loner kid, Danielle had learned that self-motivated congratulations and fun were much easier to come by than external ones. She'd spent innumerable hours deep in her mind as a pre-teen superheroine. At twenty-nine she was well on her way to becoming a real life one, though Helo-girl had never been a character she'd thought of in her youth.

External validation or not, after two years of training with the U.S. Army's 160th Special Operations Aviation Regiment she was ready for some action. At least *she* was convinced that she was. But the trainers of Fort Campbell, Kentucky had not signed off on anyone in her trainee class yet. Nor had they given any hint of when they might.

She ducked ten tons of racing Chinook under a bridge and bounced into a near vertical climb to clear the power line on the far side. Like a ride on the toboggan at Terrassee Dufferin during Le Carnaval de Québec, only with five thousand horsepower at her fingertips. Using her Army signing bonus—the first money in her life that was truly hers—to attend *Le Carnaval* had been her one trip back to her birthplace since her mother took them to America when she was ten.

To even apply to SOAR required five years of prior military rotorcraft experience. She had applied after seven years because of a chance encounter—or rather what she'd thought was a chance encounter at the time.

Captain Justin Roberts had been a top Chinook pilot, the one who had convinced her to switch from her beloved Black Hawk and try out the massive twin-rotor craft. One flight and she'd been a goner, begging her commander until he gave in and let her cross over to the new platform. Justin had made the jump from the 10th Mountain Division to the 160th SOAR not long after that.

Then one night she'd been having pizza in Watertown, New York a couple miles off the 10th's base at Fort Drum.

"Danielle?" Justin had greeted her with the surprise of finding a good friend in an unexpected place. Danielle had liked Justin—even if he was a too-tall, too-handsome cowboy and completely knew it. But "good friend" was unusual for Danielle, with anyone, and Justin came close.

"Captain Roberts," as a dry greeting over the top edge of her Suzanne Brockmann novel didn't faze him in the slightest.

"Mind if I join ya?" A question he then answered for himself by sliding into the opposite seat and taking a slice of her pizza. She been thinking of taking the leftovers back to base, but that was now an idle thought.

"Are you enjoying life in SOAR?" she did her best to appear a normal, social human, a skill she'd learned by rote. *Greeting someone you knew after a time apart? Ask a question about them.* "They treating you well?"

"Whoo-ee, you have no idea, Danielle," his voice was smooth as…well, always…so she wouldn't think about it also sounding like a pickup line. He was beautiful, but didn't interest her; the outgoing ones never did.

"Tell me." *Men love to talk about themselves, so let them.*

And he did. But she'd soon forgotten about her novel, and would have forgotten the pizza if he hadn't reminded her to eat.

His stories shifted from intriguing to fascinating. There was a world out there that she'd been only peripherally aware of. The Night Stalkers of the 160th SOAR weren't simply better helicopter pilots, they were the most highly-trained and best-equipped ones on the planet. Their missions were pure razor's edge and black-op dark.

He'd left her with a hundred questions and enough interest to fill out an application to the 160th. Being a decent guy, Justin even paid for the pizza after eating half.

The speed at which she was rushed into testing told her that her meeting with Justin hadn't been by chance and that she owed him more than half a pizza next time they met. She'd asked after him a couple of times since she'd made it past the qualification exams—and the examiners' brutal interviews that had left her questioning her sanity, never mind her ability.

"Justin Roberts is presently deployed, ma'am," was the only response she'd gotten.

Now that she was through training—almost, had to be soon, didn't it?—Danielle realized that was probably less of an evasion and more likely to do with the brutal op tempo the Night Stalkers maintained. The SOAR 1st Battalion had just won the coveted Lt. General Ellis D. Parker awards for Outstanding Combat Aviation Battalion *and* Aviation Battalion of the Year. They'd been on deployment every single day of the last year, actually of the last decade-plus since 9/11.

The very first Special Forces boots on the ground in Afghanistan were delivered that October by the Night Stalkers and nothing had slacked off since. Justin might be in the 5th battalion D company, but they were just as heavily assigned as the 1st.

Part of their training had included tours in Afghanistan. But unlike their prior deployments, these were brief, intense, and then they'd be back in the States pushing to integrate their new skills.

SOAR needed her training to end and so did she.

Danielle was ready for the job, in her own, inestimable opinion. But she wasn't going to get there until the trainers signed off that she'd reached fully mission-qualified proficiency.

The Fort Campbell training course was never set up the same from one flight to the next, but it always had a time limit. The time would be short and they didn't tell you what it was. So she drove the Chinook for all it was worth like Regina Jaquess waterskiing her way to U.S. Ski Team Female Athlete of the Year.

The Night Stalkers were a damned secretive lot, and after two years of training, she

Target of the Heart (excerpt)

understood why. With seven years flying for the 10th, she'd thought she was good.

She'd been repeatedly lauded as one of the top pilots at Fort Drum.

The Night Stalkers had offered an education in what it really meant to fly. In the two years of her training, she'd flown more hours than in the seven years prior, despite two deployments to Iraq. And she'd spent more time in the classroom than her life-to-date accumulated flight hours.

But she was ready now. It was *très viscérale*, right down in her bones she could feel it. The Chinook was as much a part of her nervous system as breathing.

Too bad they didn't build men the way they built the big Chinooks—especially the MH-47G which were built specifically to SOAR's requirements. The aircraft were steady, trustworthy, and the most immensely powerful helicopters deployed in the U.S. Army—what more could a girl ask for? But finding a superhero man to go with her superhero helicopter was just a fantasy for a lonely teenage girl.

She dove down into a canyon and slid to

a hover mere inches over the reservoir inside the thirty-second window laid out on the flight plan.

Danielle resisted a sigh. She was ready for something to happen and to happen soon.

# # #

Pete's Chinook and his two escort Black Hawks crossed into the mountainous province of Sikkim, India ten feet over the glaciers and still moving fast. It was an hour before dawn, they'd made it out of China while it was still dark.

"Twenty minutes of fuel remaining," Nicolai said it like a personal challenge when they hit the border.

"Thanks, I never would have noticed."

It had been a nail-biting tradeoff: the more fuel he burned, the more easily he climbed due to the lighter load. The more he climbed, the faster he burned what little fuel remained.

Safe in Indian airspace he climbed hard as Nicolai counted down the minutes remaining, burning fuel even faster than he had been while crossing the mountains of southern Tibet. They caught up with the U.S. Air Force

Target of the Heart (excerpt)

HC-130P Combat King refueling tanker with only ten minutes of fuel left.

"Ram that bitch," Nicolai called out.

Pete extended the refueling probe which reached only a few feet beyond the forward edge of the rotor blade and drove at the basket trailing behind the tanker on its long hose.

He nailed it on the first try despite the fluky winds. Striking the valve in the basket with over four hundred pounds of pressure, a clamp snapped over the refueling probe and Jet A fuel shot into his tanks.

His helo had the least fuel due to having the most men aboard, so he was first in line. His Number Two picked up the second refueling basket trailing off the other wing of the Combat King. Thirty seconds and three hundred gallons later and he was breathing much more easily.

"Ah," Nicolai sighed. "It is better than the sex," his thick Russian accent only ever surfaced in this moment or while picking up women.

"Hey, Nicolai," Nicky the Greek called over the intercom from his crew chief position seated behind Pete. "Do you make love in Russian?"

A question Pete had always been careful to avoid.

"For you, I make special exception." That got a laugh over the system.

Which explained why Pete always kept his mouth shut at this moment.

"The ladies, Nicolai? What about the ladies?" Alfie the portside gunner asked.

"Ah," he sighed happily as he signaled that the other choppers had finished their refueling and formed up to either side, "the ladies love the Russian. They don't need to know I grew up in Maryland and I learn my great-great-grandfather's native tongue at the University called Virginia."

He sounded so pleased that Pete wished he'd done the same rather than study Japanese and Mandarin.

Another two hours of—thank god—straight-and-level flight at altitude through the breaking dawn and they landed on the aircraft carrier awaiting them in the Bay of Bengal. India had agreed to turn a blind eye as long as the Americans never actually touched their soil.

Once standing on the deck—and the worst

Target of the Heart (excerpt)

of the kinks had been worked out—he pulled his team together: six pilots and seven crew chiefs.

"Honor to serve!" He saluted them sharply.

"Hell yeah!" They shouted in response and saluted in turn. It was their version of spiking the football in the end zone.

A petty officer in a bright green vest appeared at his elbow, "Follow me please, sir." He pointed toward the Navy-gray command structure that towered above the carrier's deck. The Commodore of the entire carrier group was waiting for him just outside the entrance. Not a good idea to keep a One-Star waiting, so he waved at the team.

"See you in the mess for dinner," he shouted to the crew over the noise of an F-18 Hornet fighter jet trapping on the #2 wire. After two days of surviving on MREs while squatting on the Tibetan tundra, he was ready for a steak, a burger, a mountain of pasta...maybe all three.

The green escorted him across the hazards of the busy flight deck. Pete had kept his helmet on to buffer the noise, but even at that he winced as another Hornet fired up and was flung aloft by the catapult.

"Orders, Major Napier," the Commodore handed him a folded sheet the moment he arrived. "Hate to lose you."

The Commodore saluted, which Pete automatically returned before looking down at the sheet of paper in his hands. The man left before the import of Pete's orders slammed in.

A different green-clad deckhand showed up with Pete's duffle bag and began guiding him toward a loading C-2 Greyhound twin-prop airplane. It was parked number two for the launch catapult, close behind the raised jet-blast deflector.

His crew, being led across in the opposite direction to return to the berthing decks below, looked at him aghast.

"Stateside," was all he managed to gasp out as they passed.

A stream of foul cursing followed him from behind. Their crew was tight. Why the hell was Command breaking it up?

And what in the name of fuck-all had he done to deserve this?

He glanced at the orders again as he stumbled up the Greyhound's rear ramp and crash landed into a seat.

Training rookies?
It was worse than a demotion.
This was punishment.

Target of the Heart *and other titles are available at fine retailers everywhere.*

Other works by M.L. Buchman

The Night Stalkers

Main Flight
The Night Is Mine
I Own the Dawn
Wait Until Dark
Take Over at Midnight
Light Up the Night
Bring On the Dusk
By Break of Day

White House Holiday
Daniel's Christmas
Frank's Independence Day
Peter's Christmas
Zachary's Christmas
Roy's Independence Day

and the Navy
Christmas at Steel Beach
Christmas at Peleliu Cove

5E
Target of the Heart
Target Lock on Love

Firehawks

Main Flight
Pure Heat
Full Blaze
Hot Point
Flash of Fire

SMOKEJUMPERS
Wildfire at Dawn
Wildfire at Larch Creek
Wildfire on the Skagit

Delta Force
Target Engaged
Heart Strike

Angelo's Hearth
Where Dreams are Born
Where Dreams Reside
Maria's Christmas Table
Where Dreams Unfold
Where Dreams Are Written

Eagle Cove
Return to Eagle Cove
Recipe for Eagle Cove
Longing for Eagle Cove
Keepsake for Eagle Cove

Deities Anonymous
Cookbook from Hell: Reheated
Saviors 101

Dead Chef Thrillers
Swap Out!
One Chef!
Two Chef!

SF/F Titles
Nara
Monk's Maze

*For new release info and exclusive extras,
sign up for his newsletter at:
www.mlbuchman.com*

Made in the USA
Middletown, DE
22 December 2016